AURELIA YATES

Warning

This book is rated R; not appropriate for readers under 18 years of age; contains elements of sex and language.

Acknowledgements

Thank you to my family, friends, my ARC group, readers and all the booktokers for your support. I couldn't do this without you.

Love to all!

Aurelia

CHAPTER ONE

THE EARLY MORNING WIND RIPS THROUGH THE AIR, shifting the blanket of snow from the frozen landscaped areas to refill the shoveled walkway I'm standing on. Some of the snow dusts onto my Berluti Oxfords, and I tap the toes of my shoes together to dislodge it. "Hurry up, William," I mutter as I wait under the portico of my penthouse complex. The sooner he brings the car around, the sooner I can get out of this cold and, hopefully, seal the deal on my next acquisition.

It's seven below zero and December has just started —we're not even into the coldest months of a Pennsylvania winter yet. No matter how cold it gets here, though, it's nothing compared to the winters I spent at boarding school in Switzerland, which lasted for six goddamn months. I swear that every time I stepped outside during those endless winters, my dick would hide, disappearing into my sack, and then my balls would freeze up. It was fucking miserable.

My parents had chosen that exclusive, all-male

boarding school so they could feel better about themselves. Every August, they'd drop me off at the airport in Philly and say, We're giving you a better opportunity than we had. Even after all these years, their words drift through my mind occasionally. Back then, each word had felt like a dagger stabbing me in the heart. They still do.

As an only child being raised by indifferent, social climbing parents, I spent a lot of time alone. My best—and pretty much only friend during my childhood and teen years was my cousin Jackson. He made coming home from boarding school each summer bearable, and he has shown up for me since then time and time again. I've no doubt his steadfast, outgoing nature is because of his mother. While our mothers are sisters, they are complete opposites. Aunt Jane is caring, warm, and everyone loves her. My mother has always been distant and cold, and she only loves herself. And my father's money and social standing. I am still baffled when I stop to consider the differences between the sisters, which I try not to do too often because it also highlights the differences between Jackson and me.

What I do ponder—all too frequently, is how the contrast between my boarding school months and my summer months seems to have been the catalyst for the disparity between my professional and personal temperaments. Being sent, young and alone, to a boarding school where most of the academic year was bitterly cold and most of the other students were as young and closed off as I was, made for a lonely existence. But I learned to survive the loneliness by isolating myself and focusing on my studies. It was almost as if the freezing outdoor temperatures during Switzerland's six months of winter seeped through my pores and froze half of my heart. The other half of my heart was kept warm first by Jackson and Aunt Jane, then by my college buddies and football teammates. It's all good, though, because this compartmentalization of my personality has worked out well for me. My icy ruthlessness has fueled my business success, while I'm still able to keep close personal friendships. Now if I could only find a woman like Jackson's Candy, one who loved me more than my money…

A shiver runs through me and I'm grateful for the distraction from my memories. I'm wearing only my suit, but it's enough. I'll be either inside the car or in an office building all day and I don't want to deal with bulky outerwear. The correctness of this decision is confirmed as I watch people scurrying around in heavy coats with their faces buried in the scarves wrapped around their necks.

Those thoughts are cut off when someone scratches at my sleeve. I glance down to see an elderly woman. I'd been so in my head I hadn't even noticed her coming up to stand beside me. Not wanting to engage, I return my gaze to the road in front of me.

"It's so cold I can't feel my nose," she says. I continue to stare straight ahead, but can sense her eyeing me. "Son, you need to put a coat on."

Not replying, I keep searching for the car. I do, however, tighten my lips. I hate how people attempt to start conversations. Fortunately for me, a van arrives, and when the door opens a man sitting inside yells out, "Gertrude!" She redirects her attention towards him and in an instant, I am standing alone once more, as I prefer it. Unless I'm with Jackson or my other friends, it's what I'm comfortable with, what I've known since childhood.

William finally pulls up and gets out to open my door.

"Good morning, William," I greet him as I slide into the backseat.

"Good morning, sir."

William has been with me for fifteen years, ever since I finished college and went to work for my father. I worked for dear old Dad just long enough to build some professional connections before leaving to start my own real estate investment firm. When I left the family business, I took William with me—we're not quite pals, but he's an exceptional employee and I do care for him. He's loyal, never tardy, and a noble father. Something my father has never even tried to be. I admire William, and I'm not the only one—his children go to great lengths to look after him. I envy their abundant love for each other. I've never had that with my father. Or my mother, for that matter. On rare occasions she tried to act like a real mother, but her attempts invariably ended abruptly, as if being motherly gave her hives.

Lucky for me, the boy I once was—the boy who sought approval, affection and attention from his parents, didn't hang around long. Before leaving for my first year at boarding school, I would have jumped off the highest cliff just to have a word of praise from either one of them. Thankfully my heart soon began to ice over and I learned to let things wash over me, to not give a fuck. That ability, which I consciously keep restricted to my business personality, gives me the upper hand when I purchase failing businesses. No matter the size of the company, whether it's a small, family-owned restaurant or a larger, corporate publishing house, it's so much easier to tear down generational structures and create unemployed workers when you don't care.

"Straight to Daniel Advertising, sir?" William asks, shaking me out of the second round of memories from my unhappy childhood.

"Yes, please, William." I settle back in my seat as William drives to a suburb just past the city limits. I'm meeting with Richard Daniel, the owner of a small, family-run advertising agency that I've been hoping to purchase for some time. Despite its excellent reputation, rumors of financial trouble surfaced soon after the death of its founder, Mr. Daniel's late wife. Now is the time to make the new owner an offer. One that I know he won't be able to refuse, since the profit from the sale, if managed wisely, will be enough for a comfortable retirement for him and seed money should his son Dylan wish to start a business. So long as it's not an advertising agency, which will be prohibited by the non-compete agreement I will insist on.

Through the window I see a billboard for Clint's Coffee Shop, next right. The sign boasts artisan coffee and outstanding Yelp reviews. I make a split-second decision and instruct William to take the exit. The truth is that I'm feeling nervous. Which, by itself, is a cause for concern, because I don't get nervous. Add to that the crazy feeling I've been having lately that something is about to happen, and a stop for artisan coffee suddenly seems the perfect reset.

William pulls into a parking space, and I unfasten my seatbelt. "This won't take long. I need to stretch my legs."

When I step out of the warm car, I'm met by frosty air carrying the aroma of freshly ground beans being brewed. It's intoxicating. Following the scent, I hurry up the short concrete path. As I reach to pull on the door handle, the door swings open and smacks me in the face.

"Shit!" I yell as I bring my hand to my cheek, which is throbbing. The pain makes my eyes water. When I pull my hand away from my cheek, I blink rapidly to clear my gaze because… yes, there are a few drops of blood on my fingertips. What the hell?

A hand gently touches my arm. Even through the fabric of my suit coat and my shirtsleeve, the touch makes my skin tingle. It takes all of one second for those tingles to form a bolt of electricity that shoots straight to my heart, as if it were trying to revive me, trying to bring the frozen half of my heart back to life. Where the hell did that fanciful thought come from? I shake my head to clear it. I don't have fanciful thoughts.

The bolt of electricity must have also awakened my senses, because my nose picks up the sweetest fragrance of cinnamon. Cinnamon. I inhale again, more deeply this time. Every particle of the scent makes my dick throb and my head dizzy. The dizziness could also be explained by the impact of the door on my skull, but it's definitely the sweet scent that's making my dick want to jump out of my pants. When a woman speaks, her voice is even sweeter than the scent of cinnamon.

"Oh lord, are you okay?" she asks with the softest Southern accent. "You're bleeding… here take this napkin."

Accepting the napkin, I bring it to my face and press it against my cheek. Despite the tingles, despite the bolt of electricity, the cinnamon scent, and her sweet voice, years of practice in self-preservation have my cold heart overriding my dick. I open my mouth to give this careless woman a good tongue lashing… Until, damn it, my gaze moves to her face and I lose my voice. She's beautiful, with hazel eyes that sparkle like the brightest stars and the most flawless, fair skin I've ever seen. Her long, raven hair is pulled up into a ponytail on the top of her head. She's short, somewhere around five-two without her heels would be my guess.

"Are you okay?" she asks again.

"Yes… yes, I'm quite all right," I answer harshly. When off kilter, armor up—another lesson in self-preservation learned at boarding school.

I've got to get my shit together. I feel like a fool for staring at her, but those hazel eyes keep catching my attention, drawing me into a trance-like state. Then I hear it. The faint sound of water splashing at my feet. I lower my gaze and see a shaggy mutt staring up at me with what appears to look like a smug grin. His leg is hiked up because he's taking a piss on my Berluti Oxfords. I feel my face scrunch up in utter disgust.

"Get your mutt off my shoes," I yell to her as I shake my abused leg and foot. "Do you realize how much these shoes cost?" I can't seem to stop the flow of words as they keep spilling out of my mouth. "That… that MUTT—"

"Excuse me," her voice rises high. "He's not a mutt. He has a name and he's a superb judge of character. Hence, that's why, when I brought him out to do his business, he chose to piss on you."

She turns her head, the quickness of the motion lifting the ends of her ponytail high enough for her hair to slap me in the face, stunning me. I watch as she pulls on the mutt's leash and storms back inside.

I stand there… frozen in place. I've never been so turned on in all my thirty-eight years. No woman has ever talked back to me like that. They normally kowtow to my voice and my bank account. The women I date usually mold themselves into what they think I like. Boredom typically occurs after several I like whatever you like statements from them and then it's time for me to move on to the next woman.

My shock at being spoken to like that changes to disbelief when it registers that she brought a dog into the coffee shop. That lasts until the door to the coffee shop opens again. This time I don't get struck. I grab the door handle and hold it open as I wait for a young couple—and their dog, to exit. Their progress is slow because they're too busy eyeing me intensely. God only knows what that shrew told everyone in there, but their judgmental looks make me feel like I'm the one who pissed on someone.

I almost forego the coffee, then decide she's not winning this battle. When I finally step inside, heat rises to my neck and makes my tie feel tight. Freaking hell! Every woman and man in the coffee shop seems to have a pet at their side and all eyes—human and non-human, are on me and giving me a murderous look. The tension in the air is so thick I could choke on it. I don't know whether to stand and wait for coffee or turn and run. A growl from the mutt who pissed on me decides the issue.

As I turn around to the door so I can make a run for it, I happen to glance at the dark-haired beauty just in time to watch her bend over to pet her mutt. Her very puffy coat doesn't disguise her perfect, round ass. She pats her mutt like he's a good boy and when she reaches into her coat pocket, my eyebrows shoot up. Pulling out a treat, she offers it to the dog. Did she just give that dog a treat for pissing on my shoe?

CHAPTER TWO

I GROAN AS I PULL THE HIDEOUS SWEATER OVER MY head. The things I am willing to do simply because Jackson asks me to.

Glancing in the mirror, I exhale in resignation. I'm going to have to leave my pride at home if I intend to wear this repulsive piece of clothing. Gold tinsel is stitched to it in a pattern that wraps around the sweater, front to back, and large plush balls of material are scattered around it. It's clearly intended to look like a Christmas tree but what it really looks like is a DIY that went horribly wrong. Candy, Jackson's wife, sent the sweater over yesterday with instructions to wear it tonight to their *Kick Off the Holiday Season Christmas Sweater Party.* I'm sure it was meant to make me fit in at the party, but it's making me look and feel ridiculous. Leave it to Candy to pick out the ugliest sweater in the whole tri-state area for me to wear.

My hands brush down the cotton material and lights start flashing. They're not just flashing, they're blinding me while they reflect in the mirror. I sneer at myself. "Hell no!"

This sweater has to be an inside joke at my expense. I can't imagine anyone wearing something like this. I pull my overcoat from my closet and put it on. The damn sweater is so bulky my overcoat won't button up. I look ridiculous! Cursing under my breath, I head to the elevator and press the button to take me to the lobby. I pray that William is already waiting out front with the car—the fewer people that see me right now, the better.

When the doorman opens the lobby door for me, I see William standing beside the car, waiting. I watch his lips curl inward, and from the tightness of his cheeks, it's obvious he is biting them to keep from laughing. I hold my head high and glare at him, silently daring him to laugh. Before I step into the car, I turn to William and throw down the gauntlet. "Good evening, William. Is there something you would like to say?" I cock an eyebrow.

He bursts out laughing, "Sir, forgive me but that Christmas sweater has got to be uglier than the one my wife picked out for me."

"Ugg," I groan. Even William's wife has better taste than Candy. "For the record, I did not pick this out. Candy picked it out."

"Oh, I see." William's eyes light up. "Then I say that sweater is perfect."

He would say that. William is a huge fan of Candy's. She always looks after him whenever he's around. Whether it's fixing him a plate of food, inviting him in to sit in the den, or buying him a gift for his birthday. She's a gracious hostess and a damn good cook, but what makes her a little scary is that she knows how to fuck with a man's ego.

"Only you would say it's perfect because one, you're not wearing this and two, she treats you like a damn king when you're around her." William's smile goes to full adoration mode.

"She reminds me of my Lydia. Always coming up with some crazy ideas. Never settling until she's made sure everything is just perfect. That girl is a sweet spirit with sass. A complete delight."

I shake my head and slide into the back. After thirty minutes, we pull into the circle drive at Jackson and Candy's. Their house is almost outside the city limits, in a quiet but still prominent neighborhood. Jackson has always preferred the slower life. Except when it came to Candy, apparently. I never would have guessed he would have set his sights on someone who once worked at a strip club.

I ring the doorbell and Jackson opens the door. He laughs at my expense, at the god awful sweater that is busting out from under my overcoat. My eyes widen at him, letting him know I'm not pleased.

"What… the hell! It looks like Candy struck again." He opens his arms wide, giving me a view of his sweater, and I am somewhat mollified. His sweater is slightly worse than mine, something I didn't think was possible.

The corner of my mouth rises. "Appears that way," I say to Jackson.

"Come in, man. Just a heads up, Candy—"

He's immediately cut off when Candy gives an excited scream as she heads our way with a more-than-pleased smile on her face.

"You look… perfect!" She claps her hands like she's proud to have picked out this god forsaken sweater.

I narrow my eyes at her. "I've been set up."

Her jaw drops, and she turns to Jackson playfully swatting his arm. "You weren't supposed to tell him."

Jackson holds up his hands. "I didn't even get the chance."

I intend to ask *Tell me what?* but I lose focus when the scent of cinnamon tantalizes my nostrils and throws me back to this morning's debacle at Clint's Coffee Shop. My back stiffens and my mouth waters because *I know that scent.* It's the same sweet scent that surrounded a very gorgeous, very irritating woman and her ill-mannered mutt.

"Dylan!" Candy screeches, rushing past me to greet the next guest arriving.

I slowly turn and am instantly mesmerized by hazel eyes. The same eyes that held a violently twisting thunderstorm in them this morning. They're so crystal clear now that I could fall into them and never want to find my way out. It's a conundrum. How can one woman make a man want to hate her and fuck her all in the same day? Whatever it is, this woman has it down to perfection.

Gone is this morning's ponytail. Her long, raven hair is now loose and being blown about by the blustery wind that has been harassing us since this morning. She takes a step inside the foyer, which brings her closer to me and makes me lose all coherent thoughts, leaving me stupid. Which is something no woman has ever done.

I registered her beauty when I saw her earlier today, but tonight I realize that she is gorgeous. My gaze zeroes in on her full, bright red lips. They are the perfect heart shape, and they'd look even more perfect if they were wrapped around something fat like my—

I jump backwards when a vision of a tiny mutt comes to the front of my mind. My eyes scan the floor, looking for a mutt to avoid. I can't risk a second pair of Berlutis getting wet. Thankfully, her four-legged terror is nowhere in sight. When I look back up, the woman has a smirk on her face, and I match hers with one of my own.

"Dylan, this," Candy waves a hand toward me, "is Jackson's cousin Shane Brown. Shane, this is my friend, Dylan Daniel."

No. It can't be. As in Daniel Advertising? As in THE Dylan Daniel that skipped out of our meeting today? I had assumed Dylan was a male, not a female. *Shit!*

"Daniel," I state her name, but it's more of a question. "As in Daniel Advertising?"

"Yes, Mr. Brown. I heard you had a meeting with my father today. I apologize for not being there. Prior engagements prevented me from attending, and I couldn't cancel them," she purrs as a tight-lipped grin appears on her face.

Prior engagements? Like needing to give treats to your dog for pissing on a stranger's shoes? I want to be sarcastic and say it, but then think better of it. Dylan is the other half of Daniel Advertising, as I'd learned this morning, and I want to make this purchase as quickly as possible. I only need her signature; her dad seems to be on board with selling to me. Nothing could be settled today, though, since Dylan wasn't at the meeting.

"I need a drink," I grunt out.

"Stay here. I'll go grab you a beer." Jackson dashes off toward the kitchen before I get the chance to object.

My eyes lock with Dylan's and I'm sure Candy feels the chill that settles in the air. The stare that Dylan and I are sharing is anything but friendly. It's the beginning of a war. It's the moment before someone yells out, *Charge!* Neither one of us is backing down, and even Candy can't break our staring contest when she clears her throat and gives a small cough. She tries again to break the silent war by laying her hand on Dylan's arm. This time she succeeds in pulling Dylan's attention away from me.

I feel a headache beginning. This woman has me tied up in knots. *Where in the hell is my beer?* I need something cold to cool down the fever this woman has started in me since apparently my ice cold heart doesn't see this as a business meeting and has taken the evening off.

"Dylan, let me grab your coat." Candy is back to her hostess-with-the-mostest persona.

"Thanks."

Dylan slides her coat down her arms revealing a snug, red sweater dress that hugs all of her curves. There's a black bow in the front at her waistline. She looks perfectly wrapped, begging for me to untie her. I shift, trying to keep my thickening dick from being too obvious.

When Candy practically runs from us with Dylan's coat in hand, we stand in uncomfortable silence. I decide if I want to purchase Daniel Advertising I need to play nice. "Where's your mutt? Is he taking a break from pissing on expensive shoes?" It appears my cold heart has shown up to this meeting after all, because the nice words I intended vanished.

Her head jerks up and her eyes look so intense that I wonder if it hurts. "He has a name. It's Mittens. USE IT!"

I snort, "Mittens."

She pushes her shoulder rather hard into me as she stomps past. I can't help but turn to watch her ass. *I should have handled that better, but the woman gets under my skin.*

"She's smart, beautiful, and can ruffle your feathers," Jackson comments in my ear. "Here," he hands me my beer. "You're going to need this liquid courage if you're interested, and you look VERY interested."

"I'm not interested," I scoff.

"Sure, you keep telling yourself that, but your face says a whole different story," Jackson laughs, taunting me.

CHAPTER THREE

Dylan

WHO DOES HE THINK HE IS? I DON'T CARE HOW much money that grumpy, arrogant prick has or how hot he is. I don't care about the height those long legs of his give him. Legs which, if the way the fabric of his pants stretches so tightly over his thighs is an indication, most likely have visible muscle definition. Nor do I care about his dark hair that he wears in a fade—shaved on the sides and just long enough on top to grab a handful to hold while he's doing things you only see in porn. Nor do I care about those blue eyes that shine like stars.

I panicked when the coffee shop door hit him in the face, worried I'd hurt him, but then he opened his mouth, obliterating any concern I may have had for him. Rude, loud, obviously rich, and, unfortunately, completely my type. The grumpy type that thinks they're entitled to everything or anything they want. The type of man you know is one hell of a fuck. The kind you run from and warn other women about if they value their self worth.

"What do you think?" Candy questions me.

"About what?"

"About Shane," she whispers. "I didn't miss the electricity between you two," she croons as she fans herself dramatically. "I thought your clothes were going to start flying through the air and your naked bodies would be slamming against the wall."

"Not happening," I say firmly.

"Why not?" Her shoulders slump. "You haven't even given him a chance."

"Oh, trust me. This morning I ran into him. Literally." Candy inches closer. "I was grabbing my normal cup of coffee at Clint's—"

Candy cuts me short. "Were there sparks?"

"You could say he saw stars," I huff, before a smile crosses my face. "When I was taking Mittens out for a potty break," I giggle, "I smacked him right in the face with the door." I laugh with madness thinking about what Mittens did to him.

"What? Tell me, what else happened. What's so funny?" Candy asks excitedly.

"Mit—," I can barely get the words out. "Mittens…" I pause trying to compose myself. "Mittens peed on his very expensive shoes." We both fold over with laughter.

"Really?" Candy chokes out.

"Oh yes. It went down like that. He then called Mittens a mutt, and my feathers stood up. I said a few words letting him have it and went back inside. Afterwards he came into Clint's and I made sure he saw me giving Mittens a treat for peeing on his shoes."

"You didn't."

"Yep. He shouldn't have called him a mutt."

Candy laughs. "I admit he's a bit frosty on the outside but when you get to know him, he's really a great guy."

"I'm sure," I drawl, because disbelief fills me.

She puts her hand on my arm, "No, he is. Every Christmas he donates tons of toys to children. He doesn't only donate at Christmas, either. He gives all year. I invited both of you in hopes that you would… maybe hook up. Sorry," Candy's eyes bleed sincerity. "I thought you two would make a great couple. Since you're into rescuing dogs and he does so much for children."

I laugh. "Jackson's dick really has changed you." She sighs as I continue. "His magic stick has gotten your head too far up in the clouds."

"You had heat in your eyes when you were looking at him, and Jackson's tree trunk has nothing to do with this."

I give her a serious look. "Those stare downs were not from heated hormones. They were a death glare. Plus, you need to stop playing matchmaker. I'm way too busy for dating."

"Oh, I'm not quite done," she promises. "Okay everyone. Listen up." Candy claps to grab everyone's attention. "We have several games we are playing tonight but first you each have to vote for who has the ugliest Christmas sweater. Jackson and I will be passing out slips of paper for you to write your vote on and I'll be collecting them. At the end of the night, we'll announce the winner."

Candy starts helping Jackson hand out slips of paper for voting. I'm the first one she hands a slip of paper to. I stare at it. *I know who has the most god awful sweater but letting him win is not happening. I'll vote for myself.* I've put my pen to my paper and am about to write my name when a deep voice breaths into my ear.

"Shane is spelled S. H. A. N. E."

I pretend to be overly excited at his spelling skills. "I'm so glad you can spell!" I click my tongue. "I was worried you might need help. Should I give you a crayon to write it down with?" I'm being sarcastic, which is so out of the norm for me. With everyone else, I'm nice, upbeat, and try to solve their problems, but this man seems to bring the worst out of me. It's his arrogance, it has to be. I bet he doesn't even wipe his own ass. He looks like the type who would call his maid to come and clean him.

He blinks like he's stunned I didn't roll out the red carpet for him.

"Listen," he holds his right hand up. "I think we got off on the wrong foot. Can we start over?"

I eye him suspiciously. *He's up to something.* "Only if you apologize for calling Mittens a mutt." I walk over to the drinks table, grab a glass and fill it with punch. When I take a sip, I almost spit it out. The taste of alcohol is so strong—it must be ninety-nine percent pure alcohol. "Who made this?" I whisper to myself.

As I set the glass down, Shane comes up behind me

and reaches over me, brushing his hard body against my backside.

"Let's both just apologize," he whispers in my ear.

"What do I have to apologize over?"

"Look at you two," Candy gushes behind us. "Look!" She points up to the ceiling. "You're standing under the mistletoe," she winks at me. *Seriously Candy?* "You have to kiss!" *No, she didn't just say that.*

I give her a look, the one I used to give her in college when she tricked me into doing things we had no business doing. My eyes shut to slits and then pop open as I give her a tight-lipped grin. She knows the look well. It doesn't do any good, though, just like it didn't work in college. She pays me no attention.

"Let's give the people what they want," Mr. Smooth breaths into my ear.

"Oh no, I'm not—" I'm cut off when Shane's lips land on mine.

His lips are so soft and plush I can't help but lean toward him. I allow myself to savor the outright, full-blown, open-mouthed war between us. His tongue swirls, dancing around mine until my knees go weak. I grab two fistfuls of his hideous sweater to keep from falling over. *My god this man can kiss.* After his onslaught, he retreats, leaving me breathless and looking up at him. He's speaking but his words are not making sense. They sound more like Charlie Brown's teacher, *wah, wah.*

He looks down at me with a smile as I remain standing, starry-eyed as a love sick teenager. I have a feeling he knew kissing him would leave me stupidified.

Is that even a word? Ugg. I don't know if I want to slap him or go back for seconds. Candy whistles, waking me out of my daze. Catcalls in the background make me cringe. *Crap, everyone saw it.*

"Now that… was a kiss!" Candy exclaims.

"You want another one, shortcake?" Shane whispers smugly.

I push against his chest, trying to put as much distance between us as possible. It doesn't do any good because the man stays planted in the same spot, looking like a smug turd. He knows he can kiss. I bet he practiced on oranges growing up. There's just no way he got those skills naturally.

CHAPTER FOUR

Shane

I'm propped up against the living room wall, staring down my next meal. Dylan doesn't notice me or else she is ignoring me. The guys are standing around me talking, but mostly it's Harrison running his mouth.

Harrison, Mitchell, and Jackson were my college roommates. Jackson and I met Harrison and Mitchell on the college's football team. We weren't the best on the team but not the worst either. What we really enjoyed were the parties, the freedom, and the girls. After our freshman year we all decided to get an apartment together and that's when we partied harder. Those were the best of days. I hardly ever had to wear my icy, ruthless mask.

"Dude, are you even listening?" Harrison nudges me.

"Yeah," I tell him without taking my eyes off Dylan.

"What did I just say?"

"You said you caught the crabs."

The guys bust out laughing with the exception of Harrison.

"Fuck right off," he bites out but I can tell there's humor to his retort. We're always jabbing jokes at each other.

"I was asking you if you wanted to meet up with Angel's friend tomorrow. But I should have known grumpy pants," he jabs his finger at me, "wouldn't want to have fun. All work and no play don't get you pussy."

"What the hell! What about me?" Mitchell slaps Harrison's chest with the back of his hand.

"Fuck no. Last time I tried to give you a girl, you took mine too. I guess I'll just have to satisfy them both."

"I can't help it if a woman happens to know a stud when she sees one," Mitchell puffs his chest out.

"More like a fuck toy," Jackson joins in.

"I'm not complaining," Mitchell says with pride. "I get what I need, they get what they want. Win, win."

"One day you're going to come across a woman who's going to have you crawling on your knees," Jackson warns him.

"Kind of like you and Shane over here."

"Huh?" I've been staring at Dylan but still managing to keep track of the jabs.

"The way you keep staring at that woman in the red dress, you might as well hand over your man card," Mitchell laughs. "I'm surprised you haven't walked over there and unwrapped her."

"She and her father own Daniel Advertising. I'm trying to purchase it."

"Damn, you can forget about hitting that then," Harrison remarks.

"Like I said, I'm only interested in her company." Everyone scoffs at my confession. Even I scoff—albeit internally.

The last thing I need is to try to bed this woman, not while she holds the key to a business deal. Yet there's something about her that has snuck past my icy professionalism and keeps drawing me in. Exhibit A is how I've pushed off the wall and am now following her down the hallway. I've been here many times before and I bet I know what room she'll go in. *Yup.* I wait outside the closed door until she begins to open it. When she has it open a few inches, I step toward the door, using my large frame to push the door open and her backward until we're both inside the bathroom. Then I shut the door and lock it behind me to secure us in.

"What are you doing?" she hisses, raising her eyebrows and tossing her hands up in the air.

I have no freaking clue what I'm doing. All I can think of is getting closer to her, being near her. The fire she has in her matches mine. I can feel it. I'm wondering if she can feel it. She has to, it's undeniable.

I try to think of something, anything to say but the words that come out are the wrong ones. "I'm offering more than a fair price for your company." *What the hell!* I did *not* mean for those words to vomit out.

Dylan folds her arms, tapping her foot as she snaps, "You can't be serious! You followed me into the bathroom to let me know how appreciative I should be because you offered my father a 'fair' price?" She makes air quotes around the word *fair,* as if suggesting it's anything but.

No. I mean yes. No, I definitely made a mistake. I'm screwed. My silence gives her the opportunity to continue slaughtering me.

"Why would we want to sell to an arrogant prick who doesn't care about anything other than money? You don't care about the people who work there. You don't care about my mother's legacy. The long, hard hours she worked to build Daniel Advertising. So excuse me if I don't feel grateful for the pittance you offered." She tries to push past me but I grab her by the shoulders and pull her body flush to mine.

"Any other man might be pissed by the character assassination you just completed. Not me, I like it." I run my nose along the top of her forehead. The scent of cinnamon is strong. I thrust my hips into her. A small gasp bolts out of that sassy mouth. "I've never seen anything hotter or sexier. You're right. I did deserve that. You make me crazy. I've done nothing but think about you ever since you almost knocked me out cold this morning. I want to kiss you but I won't do it again until you ask me." I'm not lying—I really do want to kiss her again but after the verbal flogging I just received, I think she would bite my tongue off.

She twists out of my hold and steps back. "I'm not cheap," she whispers as her eyes start to fill with tears. "You can't come in here announcing your request to purchase my mother's legacy and expect me to fall into your arms. Life doesn't work like that. Family means something. That company means something," she declares as she turns, unlocks the door and stomps out, slamming the door behind her.

I run my hands down my face. "Shit." I just screwed up this deal again.

I suspect she's right. But how would I know what family means? My parents hardly exemplified a loving family. The only person who knows what my childhood was like is Jackson. Even Harrison and Mitchell have no idea what shitty parents I have.

I inhale a deep breath before stepping out into the hallway. When I do, I look to where I left my friends. They're standing in the same place with their attention directed at me and all six eyebrows are raised to their hairlines. I'm sure everyone heard the commotion that went down in the bathroom. Maybe I should take Harrison up on his offer. I need to get laid.

CHAPTER FIVE

Dylan

I'M STANDING IN CANDY'S KITCHEN, LOOKING OUT the window over the sink into the pitch black of the night, fuming at Mr. Brown's boldness. *How dare he.* Tears stream down my cheeks and I wipe them off as fast as they fall. I need to get myself together. I'm stronger than this.

"Dylan," Candy's voice is soft.

Her hands land on my shoulders and she turns me around. My arms spread wide and I wrap myself around her. With my head on her shoulder, I let myself cry for the loss of my mother, for the loss of her companionship, but most of all for the time with her that was stolen from me.

"It's going to be okay," Candy rubs my back.

"I think… I'm going crazy."

She smiles at me, "No… well… maybe a tiny bit," she says as she holds up her thumb and forefinger. It's enough to get me to smile. "What happened?"

I roll my eyes. "Mr. Shane Brown was born."

"Come on. Tell me what's really going on. Wait… let's go and sit in the sunroom. We'll have more privacy there." Once in the sunroom, Candy sits down and pats the cushion beside her. "Sit."

I do as I'm told, but instead of sitting gracefully like a lady, I plop down. "Ugg, I don't know. It's not really him. It's the fact something is changing again. Remember I told you that our company wasn't doing well?" She nods her head. "Well, we may have to sell. Let me rephrase that. We *have* to sell."

"I thought you had gotten a loan."

"Yes, but it didn't really solve our problems. It just brought on more expenses. Our clients are going to bigger advertising agencies that have more pull and who don't pay their employees decent wages. It used to be that our name meant something to people. They knew with us they would get the best treatment. That's not enough anymore to keep them coming back. The customers just want more and more production from us without price increases, and providing those services costs more than what we are profiting."

It's been four days since Candy's party and I've done everything I can to keep myself busy and avoid thinking about Shane Brown and his condescending ways. He did lose the attitude after I lost my shit on him, I have to give him that. Truthfully, he avoided me for the rest of the night. A part of me felt bad, and I was tempted to apologize. Give him a chance. He *did* look nervous as hell when he stepped into the bathroom. But then he opened his mouth and the words he spewed… He was back to his self-serving ways. *Asshole.*

An asshole that kisses like a fucking rockstar! Holy shit that kiss we shared earlier that night under the mistletoe was hotter than any kiss I've ever had. Which makes me wonder: What the hell is wrong with me? Am I really going crazy? I shouldn't be so attracted to him. If he wasn't trying to steal my mother's company, I would have been climbing him during that kiss. Especially since it's been some time since I've had any sex. But nope. With things as they are, I can't let myself go there.

I toss my pen down on my desk and close my eyes. The exquisite kiss under the mistletoe plays in my mind again, making my core heat up. It's the only kiss that has ever left me weak in the knees. It was a once-in-a-lifetime, earth-moving experience. His lips were soft, yet so full of power. I bet he could suck the peel right off an apple. *I take back my thought at the party… he probably practiced on apples, not oranges.* Why do I let myself daydream of him? The man is trying to buy my mother's company, her dream. If that isn't bad enough, my dad *wants* to sell because we both know mother was the backbone of the company and we're losing money every day just trying to keep the lights on.

Knock, knock. My office door opens. "Hey honey," my dad greets me.

"Hey Dad."

"Do you have a moment?"

"For you, anytime. Come on in." When he sits down, I take in his features. I don't how, but he looks like he's aged since I saw him yesterday.

"We need to talk about the offer we got a few days ago."

I deflate in my seat. I knew this was coming but I was hoping a miracle would fall into our lap. I tried to get another loan, but we're maxed out on our credit. Jason Moore, the bank's president, did everything he could do to help but in the end it wasn't enough. This deal my father is wanting to talk about is the one we received from Shane. He offered enough to pay off our bills and for Dad to retire. It just hurts to sell the company my mom built. And our employees are also my friends… I can't take away their incomes.

"As bad as I hate it, I know we have to sell." My eyes are cast down. "Selling feels like we're disappointing Mom."

"You're not," my dad says sternly.

Tears cloud my eyes. "It feels like it."

"Let me tell you a secret," Dad says as he leans back in the chair and crosses one leg over the other. "Your mother cared about this company but she loved being a mother and a wife more. This," my dad swirls his finger in the air, "was not what made her happy. *You* were what made her happy. Before she passed, she told me to sell. She knew that running the company wasn't what I wanted to do but that I would want to keep it going as a way to hold on to a piece of her and also as an inheritance for you. But your mom was a wise woman, and she told me that holding on to her memory doesn't mean not selling the company, because it's what's in our hearts that keeps her memory alive."

Dad stands up and rounds the corner of my desk. "It's time. This company was her dream, not yours. And now you need to find your dream and live it. Your mother would've wanted that. So take some time off. We're not in a hurry to sign the papers. We can sign after Christmas," he finishes, bending down to kiss me on the forehead.

When he leaves my office, I exhale, releasing some of the tension in my chest. I've been so stressed about the company's downfall that I haven't taken any time off in over a year. All that mattered to me was saving this place. Maybe Dad's right and some time off would be good for me. It'll give me time to decide if I truly want to let go of the company or make a decision to fight. And if I were to fight, would I be fighting for something that mattered to me? Something that I would be happy to do every day for the rest of my life?

THE NEXT MORNING, I LAY IN BED, STARING UP AT the ceiling and wondering what the hell I'm going to do today. I haven't taken a day off in so long that I don't know what free time is. Mittens jumps on the bed, wagging his tail.

"You need to go potty, sweet boy?" I laugh out loud. The image of Mittens peeing on Shane's shoe will always be stuck in my mind. Mittens jumps on top of me, excited about going out. "Do you want to wear your Christmas sweater?" Mittens barks. "Yes you do, don't you?"

I get up, dress, and pull Mittens' sweater over him. Once I've put on my coat and boots, I grab his leash and we're out the door. Mittens goes potty like a good boy and then we walk to Clint's, my favorite coffee shop. Not only is the coffee excellent, but it's pet friendly. Mittens enjoys socializing there as much as I do.

Clint's is a few blocks from my house and it doesn't take us long to get there. The walk is always pleasant, with each neighbor saying *Good morning* as they sweep off their sidewalks. Our neighborhood is older, with mature oak trees that stand tall along the sidewalks. The houses are colonial style and almost as old as the oak trees. I couldn't have chosen a better place to live.

When we walk in, the usual crowd is sitting at their usual tables.

"Good morning, Dylan," the barista calls to me. I've been coming here for the past three years, ever since I purchased my home. "Do you want your usual?"

"Yes, please."

Mittens stands beside me, his eyes and ears focused toward the back of the small coffee shop. His fur is standing up and he's in attack mode. I follow his line of sight and see someone sitting at a table next to the wall. It appears to be a man, but he's holding a newspaper up to hide his face. Whoever it is sinks down into his seat.

When he docs, his feet shift from under the table enough for me notice his shoes. Oh crap! It's Shane.

An employee calls my name, signaling for me to pick up my Earl Gray and lavender tea. My hand reaches for the tea just as Mittens starts barking and pulling on the leash, distracting me.

CHAPTER SIX

Shane

I CALLED DYLAN'S FATHER FIRST THING THIS morning, even before I left my condo, to try to reschedule the meeting. He informed me that Dylan was off until after the holidays and the meeting would have to wait. I suppose it makes sense for her to want to be off, to give herself time to get used to the idea of selling. I know that isn't the outcome Dylan wants mainly because she bit my head off at Jackson's party to prove that point, but they're downing in debt. She really has no choice.

After talking with her father, I decide to try to track her down and get back in her good graces. I give William the day off and call my assistant and ask him to reschedule my appointments for today. Then I scour my closet for my most non-threatening clothes, finally settling on jeans and the only flannel shirt I own. Then I drive myself to Clint's, hoping she is a creature of habit.

When I arrive, Clint's is busy, a little crowded with

both people and canines. A table in the back corner is open, so I pick up my order and head that way. I'm reading the daily newspaper—yes, I prefer to get my news the old school way, so sue me—enjoying my caramel brûlée latte, when the door opens. Both my back and my dick stiffen at the first sweet hint of cinnamon that rushes into the shop. There's no doubt who just walked in the door. Even though my purpose in coming here was to run into her, I raise my newspaper higher to hide myself. The battle inside my mind plays out. I should talk to her, but the other half of my brain urges caution: *Leave it.* I don't listen to it.

Before I know it, I'm on my feet heading in her direction. Her damn dog starts barking at me, but I ignore him. She doesn't have time to look up before I reach out and take her cup, handing it to her. Stepping back, I give her a smile when she finally looks up at me.

"Would you care to join me?" I'm on my best behavior. After our second encounter took a turn and became worse than our first, I want to make things better. Although it took me a while to figure that out, since feelings of reconciliation are not something I'm used to having. This is all new to me and I'm trying my best not to screw it up. There's also the fact that the mere *thought* of this woman makes my dick hard.

"Mittens, hush!" She turns to me. "I have plans."

"Really?" I don't doubt she does.

"Yes, not that it's any of your business but I'm volunteering today at Happy Tails Rescue Shelter."

She turns to leave but I step in front of her. "I was about to head there as well. Maybe, I can give you a lift." *What the fuck! Why did I say that? This woman and her cinnamon scent are fucking with my brain.* Dylan gives me the biggest smirk I've ever seen on any woman or man. She's about to call me on my bullshit. I just know it. "What I meant to say was that I'm going to be passing it and I could drop you off." I clear my throat, hoping she buys my sorry explanation.

"Hold on one second. I need to make a phone call." She throws her hand up and steps away.

What have I gotten myself into? I start rubbing my forehead as I look down at the floor. It's a habit I have when I get nervous. Mittens is sitting up, looking at me, and I swear the dog has a smirk on his face. I almost growl to show him who the alpha is.

"Okay, let's go. Tee put you down to volunteer as well."

"No, I—" She cuts me off.

"You wouldn't want to disappoint me, now would you?" The question hangs in the air like the bad smell of dog shit on the bottom of a shoe.

"No, ma'am. Let's go."

"You need to take me home first so that I can drop off Mittens. It will only take a minute. Don't plan on inviting yourself in," she says with a smirk.

I'm grateful for her plan. While she's getting Mittens settled, I Google *Happy Tails* to see where the hell it is. Since I said I was headed that way, I should look like I know where I'm going.

Once we get to the shelter, Dylan goes to the front desk and asks for her friend, Tee. The young girl at the desk tells her that Tee is in the back.

"I'll be right back," Dylan informs me.

I nod, acknowledging her. Dylan opens the door that I assume leads to the back and the noise level goes up at least ninety decibels. By the sound of it, they must have a hundred dogs back there. It's not long before Dylan emerges with someone I'm guessing is Tee.

The lady sticks her hand out and I'm proven correct. "Hi, I'm Tee." We shake hands because it would be rude as hell if I didn't. "I'm so glad you decided to volunteer today." I don't inform her that it wasn't my idea. I just keep my mouth closed and give her a half smile and a nod. "We were supposed to have a couple more volunteers today but they didn't show, so having you and Dylan surprise us is wonderful."

I give Dylan the side eye. Was she not on the schedule? I bet the phone call she made at Clint's was to arrange this little test for me. *Game on, baby.*

"Shane really wants to works with the dog kennels," Dylan says. There's no mistaking the wicked glee on her face.

"That would be so great!" Tee is thrilled.

I slit my eyes at Dylan. She looks at Tee and I'm sure some secret code passes between them. Then Dylan giggles and as the sound vibrates through the air, I realize that it's official. I'm getting screwed on this deal. But to hear Dylan's carefree laugh, I decide that whatever the cost, it's worth it.

Tee leads us to the back. "Dylan, you've been here so often I'm sure you can show Shane what to do. Just remember to lock the kennels when you're finished with each animal. We had a teen volunteer about a month ago who didn't lock the kennels. Then his cell phone went off with a high-pitched ring making all the dogs go crazy. Every one of them escaped. Running the aisles, barking, and some even crapped on the floors. It was crazy."

Dylan laughs.

"Sounds like a nightmare," I mutter.

"It was," Tee says looking exhausted just from the memory.

She leaves us and we start to work. Dylan escorts each animal out with tender care. I have to admit I'm a little jealous as they get her smiles and affection. I wonder if I got down on all fours if she would treat me better than she does now… then decide probably not.

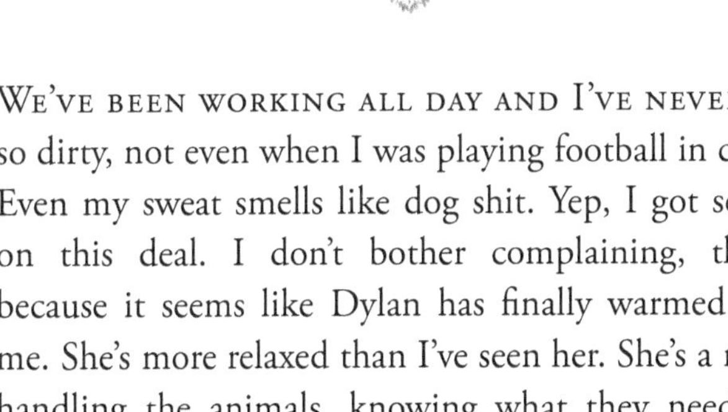

WE'VE BEEN WORKING ALL DAY AND I'VE NEVER FELT so dirty, not even when I was playing football in college. Even my sweat smells like dog shit. Yep, I got screwed on this deal. I don't bother complaining, though, because it seems like Dylan has finally warmed up to me. She's more relaxed than I've seen her. She's a natural handling the animals, knowing what they need from her. She gives some more love and care and others she handles with a firmer hand. All day long we both steal glances at each other. It gives me hope that maybe she'll see me as more than someone trying to take her mother's company from her family.

One more kennel needs to be cleaned before we call it a day. It's a large kennel with a large ass dog. A German Shepard and lab mix named Skyler. I'm ready to bolt when I see what's inside his kennel. *Damn this!*

"Oh my," Dylan laughs while she places her hand on my upper arm. I've got my nose turned up and my lips curled inward, hoping my face shows my disgust. "That's a ton of poop." She laughs even harder at my expense.

"I think I'm done for the day. This one is yours," I mutter.

"Oh no, you don't. You have to see it through." She takes Skyler by the leash and heads for the door to the play yard.

"Shit," I mutter to myself. "Literally."

The smell hits me like a brick to the face. "What the hell are they feeding him?" I yell out. There's crap everywhere. It's on the floor of the kennel, the walls, and there's even some on the ceiling of the kennel. Someone must have put a stick of dynamite up his ass to get this effect.

I man up and bend down to go through the door, but I misjudge where I step and slip on a turd, landing right in the middle of the mess. It's on my clothes and hands now. "Fuckkk," I sling my hand trying to get it off but that only makes it fly off and slap me in the face. I groan. Laughter rings in my ears.

"What..." Dylan is laughing so hard that her words are barely forming together. "How—?"

"Don't. Don't say anything," I give her in warning. Animals and I don't mix. I've never met one that liked me or that I liked. Even as a child I never got along with any dog or cat, not even any fish. I have to roll over onto all fours to get up because my hands and feet keep slipping out from under me. I'm having no luck with trying to get up, so I grab a hold of the steel mesh on the sides and pull myself up.

Dylan stands there watching me, trying to hold back more laughter. Skyler is at her side tilting his big head and probably wondering what could possibly be the problem.

I point to him. "You did this," I scold him. "You," I say again because I'm not sure he understands that he should've done his business outside.

Slipping and sliding, I finally make it up and out of the kennel. I spot a sink and make a bee line for it. When I catch my reflection in the mirror above the sink I have to look twice. Gone is the hard ass, suit-wearing professional. The man staring back at me doesn't look like me—his hair is a mess, he's wearing a flannel shirt for god's sake, and is that… Fuck me, there's a smear of dog shit on my cheek.

Then I hear giggles coming from a few feet away and I have to smile. The man in the mirror looks like a man who would clean shit for a woman he's falling HARD for. The giggles continue, reverberating through me and filling me with a warm, soft feeling. I want to bottle up the sound to replay it for later. How did I get to this point? The more important question is what the hell am I going to do to stay in her good graces?

CHAPTER SEVEN

Dylan

Candy and I are sitting at a table at our favorite café eating lunch. The sun is shining through the windows and the atmosphere inside is busy with people talking and laughing, making it seem like a warm summer day. Or, more likely, it's the subject of our conversation that keeps warming my insides. I can't stop myself from smiling when I speak his name. The one man I never would have believed I could fall for has somehow found a special place in my mind and captured a piece of my heart.

"I can not believe Shane Brown cleaned dog poop," Candy shakes her head with laughter.

It's been a couple of weeks since Shane and I first volunteered at the animal shelter. To my surprise, he's been back with me every time I've gone. I can tell he's enjoying it as much as I am. When we finish for the day, we separate, then meet up again later in the evening to have dinner together. He's not as arrogant as I had expected; instead, I'm positive there are scars from his childhood that he tries desperately to hide. It's oddly endearing.

When we're together, conversation flows easily between us. I believe that's one of his best qualities. He's just so easy to talk to. Before Shane, the men I dated usually get straight to asking for a fuck after we have dinner. As if a woman is supposed to put out just because you buy her a steak or a lobster dinner, or even a freaking hotdog. Shane hasn't tried to kiss me since Candy's party. At first I was grateful for him being a gentleman, but now I wouldn't mind having a replay of the kiss that made my toes curl.

"Earth to Dylan," Candy snaps her fingers in front of my face, trying to pull me out of my trance.

I clear my throat, "I'm back."

"Where did you go?"

I let out a breath. "I was reminiscing about the last couple of weeks. How different Shane is from my initial impression of him."

Candy reaches across the table and places her hand on mine. "I told you he wasn't bad. Sure, all men have hangups, but we do too," she relays with wisdom and smiles. "Have you guys, you know…" She wiggles her eyebrows.

"No. I've given him the chance to kiss me. Several times. Could I be reading this wrong? He's probably being nice because he wants to purchase our company."

"I've thrown out hints to Jackson to see if I can get him to tell me how Shane feels. Nothing. Men," she scoffs as she rolls her eyes. "They wouldn't know a hint if it was printed on a poster attached to the front of a Mack truck that was running them over."

"Agree…" I replay our encounter in the bathroom, searching for clues to his seeming reluctance to kiss me, when a memory makes me sit up straight. "Oh my gosh!"

"What?" Candy asks, her eyebrows knitted with concern.

"The night of your party, when we were arguing in the bathroom, he said he wouldn't kiss me again until I asked for it. And I haven't asked." I sigh. "We've been together so often lately that asking now will seem awkward."

Candy is quiet for a moment before she suddenly booms out, "I've got it!" She is vibrating with excitement. "You need mistletoe and a sexy outfit!"

I scrunch my brows and ask, "Why would I need mistletoe?"

"Invite him over and then greet him wearing a sexy outfit with a skirt, preferably with no panties." She winks. "Hang the mistletoe over your waist inviting him to camp out in your skirt." She acts like she just discovered a cure for cancer.

"I don't know, Candy. That's bold, maybe too bold for me. What makes you think that would be something he would be interested in—camping in my skirt? I know now that I'm supposed to ask, but he's not even hinted about wanting to kiss me again."

"Trust me. I can tell from the way he looks at you. I saw the heat in his eyes at our Christmas sweater party."

I tsk at her. "The so-called heat that night was fueled by hate."

"No, it wasn't. It was the same look Jackson gives me," she sighs. She opens her purse, reaches in, and pulls out a handful of candy canes that she slides in front of me. "Jackson loves candy canes! He sucks—."

"Oh god. Don't say anymore. I already know where you're going with this," I instruct as I cover my ears and shut my eyes. If I can't hear or see her, she'll stop, I tell myself. The last thing I want to hear about is Candy spread out with Jackson harvesting her.

When I dare to open my eyes, Candy is sitting there with a dreamy look on her face. It makes me shift in my chair, because for the first time I'm jealous over my friend. I want what she and Jackson have. Why shouldn't I be bold? I need to go after what I want, damn it. My feet hit the floor, ready to take me to find the perfect outfit for tonight.

"Come on. I need something sexy to wear." I grab Candy's hand and drag her out of the café.

"Shit," I jerk my hand back from the hot baking dish. The potholders I have are old and worn thin, making it easy for the heat from the dish to burn me. I would toss them, but they were my mother's. I grab a hand towel to use instead, pull the baked lasagna out of the oven and set it on a trivet on the counter.

Then I put the foil-wrapped garlic bread into the oven, turning off the heat so it warms but doesn't cook. Shane will be here soon.

The doorbell chimes, making me curse again. I wanted to have ten more minutes so I could make sure I look desirable. Mittens runs to the door, barking, while I quickly run to the hall bath and fluff up my hair and straighten my crop top and flirty red mini-skirt. I give myself one last look before heading to the door.

"Calm down, Mittens," I scold as I bend over to pick him up. Once I've got a good hold on Mittens, I open the door. *Ho-ly shit!*

Shane is standing there, tall and broad shouldered, with his hair perfectly styled. He's wearing a dark blue t-shirt that hugs his shoulders and brings out the color in his eyes. The man is gorgeous. He lets his eyes roam over me, and I watch as they fill with lust. Maybe Candy was right. My outfit might be just the ticket I need to get that kiss I want. *And maybe even more...*

"Shall I turn around and give you the complete view or do you want to come in?" I tease.

His bright blue orbs turn dark, and I've known him long enough to recognize that there's a storm brewing behind them. Every step he takes forward I match with one step back. He slams the door shut as soon as he's through the doorway, then—is he for real? He toes off his snowy shoes and sets them on the mat by the door before he stands and continues his slow stalking toward me. Mittens growls at him from his perch in my arms, no doubt trying to protect me. *Crap!* I need to give Mittens the old heave-ho before he completely kills the moment. Shane stops and doesn't make another attempt to move forward.

"Let me put him in the spare room," I say as I turn and head down the hallway.

In the spare room, I set Mittens on the bed and give him a pat on the head. "Be a good boy." Then I leave the room, closing the door behind me. I take a deep breath and walk as calmly as I can back to Shane.

I find him in the family room, taking in all of the pictures on my shelves and walls. "Are you hungry?" My voice sounds lower than normal, no doubt because of the lust clogging my throat.

His dark eyes flash to me. "Yes," he says, his voice also deeper than usual. It heats up my core.

"I'm just finishing up in the kitchen."

"Let me help. Whatever it is smells good."

"Thank you. There are only a few dishes I make really well, and lasagna is one of them. It was my mom's recipe."

Shane follows me into my small kitchen. I take the garlic bread from the oven, empty the packet into a wicker basket I've lined with a pretty cloth and hand the basket to him. "Will you take this into the dining room, please? Everything else is ready, so you can go ahead and sit down."

I grab the towel I'm using instead of potholders, lift the heavy lasagna dish, and carry it to the table. As I'm setting it down, the towel slips a bit. I recover quickly, but my elbow jostles a wine glass and it tips over and falls... shattering when it hits the hardwood floor. "Shit," I cry out. "Dinner will obviously be delayed a moment," I say as I leave the room to get the broom and dust pan.

Tiny pieces of glass are spread across the floor and I hurry to sweep them up. In my haste to clean up and get to the "highlight" of the evening, I forget Candy's plan and bend over to sweep the shards into the dust pan. Two things occur simultaneously: I feel a breeze on my lady bits and hear Shane's sharp inhale from behind me. *Oops.*

"Fuckkk," Shane whispers.

I close my eyes, mortified, because I know what he's looking at. The skirt I have on doesn't cover a damn thing when I bend over. And since I followed Candy's instructions, I'm giving him a full view of what my momma gave me. Although it was my plan to eventually make him aware of my lack of panties—the key word being *eventually,* I had hoped for a more romantic moment than while I was picking up after my clumsiness.

Groaning,I squat to finish cleaning up the broken glass. Shane growls as I stand and slowly walk to the trash can that's under the kitchen sink. I stand there, my back to him, praying that my blush will have subsided by the time I have to face him again. I had wanted to catch his attention and indeed I did!

CHAPTER EIGHT

Shane

My dick is as hard as a hammer and I'm about to combust with the need to nail Dylan to the counter. Fuck me. She's not wearing any panties under her skirt. I growl when she stands up, then watch as she walks toward the kitchen sink… and just stands there, her back to me, as if she's waiting. As if she knows she about to get it—HARD.

"Fuck me, Dylan," I murmur as I close the distance between us and stand behind her, my hands on her hips so I can press my cock firmly against her ass. She gives me a small moan, which I choose to accept as consent to continue. "Did you decide to not wear panties because you wanted to show me that sweet pussy?" My ragged breathing sounds desperate even to my own ears.

I wrap one arm around her, then use my other hand to take the dust pan and slide it onto the counter beside the sink. I remove the broom from her other hand and let it fall to the floor. "Dinner can wait. Right now we have to deal with the problem I have in my pants."

She doesn't comment, only leans into me even more. Arching her back, she pushes her ass harder into my cock. My hand goes to her exposed thigh. "Tell me if you want me to stop," I whisper into her hair as my hand slides up her thigh. When she doesn't stop me, I run my hand all the way up until I feel the warmth that is radiating off her pussy. My finger dips in between her folds. "Oh baby, you're wet. So wet for me," I growl into her ear. I step back a little, pulling her with me, to give her room to follow my next instructions. "Spread your legs and bend over to give me another perfect view of that sweetness." My needy woman bends at the waist, letting her head drop. Her raven hair falls, sweeping the floor.

Foreplay has always been a favorite game of mine. But right now, I don't think I can wait any longer. I'm about to come in my pants just from looking at her little pink pussy and the juices coating her inner thighs. No woman has ever made me want to skip eating pussy, not until this woman. I've done my best to keep my heart out of sex—and it hasn't been difficult since every woman before Dylan wanted my bank account more than she wanted me. But Dylan is different. Her reluctance to sell the company and her behavior these past weeks as we've worked together at the shelter make me think she likes *me*—the man, not the money. So what I'm about to do with her feels like more than sex. It feels like ownership. Once I have her, she's mine.

My hands can't work fast enough to unfasten my belt. "Brace yourself, baby. I'm about to fuck you… hard." The silence is broken only by the sound of my zipper sliding down and then the soft swishing of fabric as my pants and underwear drop to the floor. I step out of them, then pull my shirt off. She reaches for the zipper on her skirt but I grab her wrist. "No, I want you just like this." My voice is raspy, full of raw lust. "I'm clean. Can I take you bare?"

"Yes. I'm clean too." Her knuckles are white from the tight grip she has on the edge of the sink. She's bracing herself, ready for me. When she looks back and sees my heavy cock, her eyes go wide.

"All for you," I say. She needs to know she'll be the only one I'm fucking for the rest of my life.

I line myself up, then run the head of my cock though her folds and back up to her ass, pressing it against her tight hole. I'm not going to take that hole tonight, but it won't be long before I will have fucked every hole she has. She's mine. Pressing my cock against her entry, I still for a moment, then slide my hand under her top and rub it up her spine for reassurance. "I'm not going to be gentle. You ready?" She gives me a nod.

I slam into her in one quick movement, burying myself so far into her there's no doubt that we are now one. "Oh fuckkk," I manage to grind out through my clenched teeth. "You're so wet and tight." I'm not going to last, she feels too good. Her warmth squeezes me so tightly. I shouldn't feel the need to take her this hard, not the first time, but there's a primal beast inside of me. It's restless and wants—*needs,* to show her that no matter what happens with her company, she'll be screaming my name every night from now on.

Dylan fell asleep last night tucked securely in my arms, her head on my chest, and apparently stayed that way because she's still in the same position. Although I slept well with her beside me, I'm naturally an early riser and my mind is already sorting through my task for today. I lay in her bed for a few more minutes, feeling her breath skipping across my skin, leaving goosebumps behind as it travels over me. She's even more beautiful when she's so relaxed. Her long, raven hair is spread across my shoulder and fans over the covers. I want to stay here, just like this, all day. But I need to go in to the office to finalize the proposal I plan to offer to Mr. Daniel next week. It must be done today, so my lawyers have time to review and approve it before it's actually delivered.

Dylan stirs beside me and I use the opportunity to pull my arm from around her. When she rolls over to face the opposite wall, I slip out of bed carefully so as to not wake her. Once I've dressed, I leave her a note telling her I'm headed in to the office and will call her later. Before I head out, I sneak one last look at my sleeping beauty.

On the drive to my office, my mind races in happy anticipation of how Dylan is going to react to the arrangement I've made with her father. When I arrive, I park in my normal spot and head up. It's Saturday, so the office is quiet. I pull off my shirt as I walk into my office and head straight to the private shower.

Once I'm out and dressed in the extra set of clothes I keep here, I sit at my desk and open my computer. I'm about to get started when my phone buzzes. I press the speaker button so I can work at the same time.

"Mitchell."

"Hey man. We haven't heard from you or seen you since Jackson's party. Did you fall into a hole somewhere?" He laughs at his own joke.

"No fucker, I've been busy." I smile, thinking of the time I've spent with Dylan since the Christmas party.

"Busy getting laid, I hope."

"What are you calling me about? I'm busy."

"It's Saturday. Why in the hell are you working today?"

"I've got shit to do. Why in the hell are you calling me?"

"Would that shit be a dark haired beauty?"

"Maybe," I smile as I type my password.

Mitchell chuckles. "We're getting together at the club minus Jackson. He's pussy whipped now."

I'm starting to get it, the reason Jackson never wants to go out to party anymore. He's got everything he needs at home. A warm bed with a woman he cares about. I want that, too. Instead of telling Mitchell that, I wave it off.

"I can't. I've got too much work to finish up before my meeting next week."

Mitchell scoffs at my obvious lie. The truth is, I would rather have Dylan wrapped around me. The vision of her on her knees or lying on her back, legs spread open, is a much more tantalizing thought than the idea of watching strippers at a club where the women only want to be around you when you're handing them bills. I've had my share of strippers but that was before Dylan. She is someone I can see myself settling down with.

"I think someone else is getting pussy whipped," he jokes. "Did you unwrap her gift? We are talking about the beauty that was at Jackson's party, right? The one in the red dress with the black bow? The woman you said you were only interested in for her company?" The last sentence he drew out, no doubt teasing me for trying to convince the guys I was only interested in buying her company. My comments at the party were simple self-preservation—Mitchell and Harrison are part blood hound, and if they sniff out your interest in someone they'll fucking tease the shit out of you. All because they are players who never plan to settle down.

"I might have given *her* pussy a whooping." I try to come off as casual, just talking smack, because Mitchell is so predictable. Next, he'll be giving me his usual advice, which is to run.

"That's my boy! Now you know what to do after you buy her company? Run like hell. Women see you coming back for seconds, they start getting the idea of forever."

"I'm buying the company, so there's no running just yet. I'd be a fool to. I can benefit from their client list." It's half the truth, but Mitchell doesn't have to know that.

"So this is what you're working on?"

"Yep," I lean back and prop my feet up on my desk. "Just going over the contract now. I want to make sure everything's covered." Which is not an outright lie… I just don't bother telling him there's been some changes to the structure of the purchase. What I do is my business.

"If you get bored later, you know where to find me. I'll be the one getting my dick sucked." He hangs up, not sparing another word. Thank fuck!

It takes me a moment after Mitchell hangs up to realize I'm no longer the only one in my office. Dylan stands in the doorway with her arms folded. I've no idea how she got into the building, and the thought crosses my mind that I'll have to speak with security. That is, if I live through these next few minutes—from the anger frozen on her face, I know that I'm screwed!

"Dylan—" She cuts off my explanation by raising her hands, palms toward me, each hand silently shouting *Stop!*

"Don't talk to me. Don't call me. Don't come by to see me." She fires off each sentence sharp and fast, like bullets. "I thought you were different than the first impression I had of you. I was wrong. You are *exactly* who I thought you were." She turns on her heels and walks out. I'm too stunned to move.

I've really fucked up.

CHAPTER NINE

Dylan

"Good morning, Ms. Daniel," my assistant greets me when I exit the elevator.

"Morning, Karen." I take a deep breath as I walk past her desk, praying I can hold everything together until I get to my office.

She grabs her notebook, then follows me. "Your dad called. He wanted to make sure you remembered you have a meeting at nine with Mr. Brown. Mr. Daniel will be at the dentist, but he'll be back in time to do the meeting with you."

"Of course he will," I say with a huff.

I've ignored Shane at every turn possible. I barricaded myself in my house over Christmas. I didn't answer his calls, his text messages, or even the door when he showed up at my house. After hearing him on the phone with his friend, I don't want anything to do with him. All the time we spent together at the shelter, the dinners we shared—especially the dinner at my place, the almost constant texting and then talking most nights on the phone, I thought maybe, just maybe, he had real feelings for me. But hearing him talk about using me to buy my mother's company was an eye opener. Or maybe it'd be more appropriate to compare it to a stab in the back. Or to my heart.

Some people are just as they first appear. They may be able to fake it, if it serves their purpose, but they don't really change. Shane is one of them. He'll always be self-absorbed, looking out only for himself. I'm so angry—both at him and his tactics, but also at myself for being so damn naïve.

Karen continues, oblivious to my inner turmoil. "He also said if he doesn't make it in time, you should start without him."

The thought of being in the same room as Shane makes my stomach flip. My dad and I made the decision to sell together. It was the best option, our only option. It will get us out of debt and will give my dad enough to retire. Shane was generous with his offer, but I would never tell him that. I would rather be set on fire in the desert during the hottest months of the year than give him the satisfaction of hearing those words. *Prick!*

"When Mr. Brown arrives, show him to the board room."

Karen nods her understanding then leaves, closing the door behind her. I get started on packing up my office.

As I lift the art work off the walls, I realize that a part of me is becoming excited for the change. I've decided to go back to school to become a veterinarian. It's always been my dream to open up my own clinic.

Ever since I was a small girl, I've wanted to take care of animals. Now it looks like I can make my dream a reality. It just hurts to let go of my mother's dream.

I've taken down all of the art work in my office and started to empty the desk drawers when Karen pops her head back into the office. "Mr. Brown is waiting."

Every time his name is mentioned I want to slap myself for the way my body reacts. How my heart rate and breathing pick up whenever I hear his name spoken out loud. How my mind recalls the night we spent together, remembering every kiss and touch, and how his hands felt on my body. I need to calm myself down before I go in there. I can't walk into the board room with my hormones in full season.

"Is my father back?"

"Yes, he's in there now with Mr. Brown. Mr. Daniel is the one who sent me to get you."

I give her a slight smile. "Thank you. I'll be there in just a moment." She doesn't say anything else. It may be because of shock, since she's looking around the office, noticing, I'm sure, that it is bare of the personal items that once were on the walls and shelves.

I reach in the box in front of me and take out a pen. "Let's do this," I pep talk myself.

The board room has glass walls. So there's no hiding from anyone when I turn the corner and walk to the double glass entry doors. Shane is the first to look my way. I can't tell if his expression is one of regret because I caught him or admiration that I'm sticking to my resolve to cut him out of my life. While his attention is solely fixed on me, I notice that my father and a man I assume is Shane's lawyer exchange looks before they each then focus on me.

Opening the door, I sit as far from Shane as possible.

"Dylan, I've read over—"

I cut my father off, "No need, Dad. Just pass me what I need to sign. I have a ton of work to finish up before today is over."

Shane's lawyer hands me papers stacked together with Post-it notes sticking out. "Your father has already signed, so we just need your signature beside his," he says in a monotone as he flips though the pages, pointing his finger at each blank line for me to sign.

Meanwhile, I feel Shane staring a hole in me with those blue eyes of his. The same blue eyes that I looked into one intimate night. I remember thinking then that I wanted nothing more but to look into them every night. *It seems like so long ago.*

As I quickly sign beside the final Post-it, I ask, "Okay, that's it?"

"Yes, I wanted—"

I cut the suit off. "My dad can take care of the rest." I push myself back from the table and exit with my heart hammering in my chest. I swear, that man.

As I turn the corner, my shoulders relax in relief that it's finally over. With any luck, that will be the last time I see Shane. Or not, because before I reach the safety of my office, a large hand reaches out and takes a hold of my wrist. "Can we talk? I just want to explain."

I stop and turn to stare into his eyes. Those damn blue eyes. "No need to explain. I understand. You wanted something and you got it. Win win for you." I jerk my hand loose from his grip while backing away from him. "Don't worry about it. It meant nothing to me either." His face falls as each verbal knife I've thrown lands with precision. *Good. Let him see how it feels to be hurt so badly.*

Back in my office, I shut and lock the door before collapsing in the nearest chair. I half expected him to follow, but he didn't. A ping of guilt hits me for saying he meant nothing to me, because that was a total lie. The truth is that our short time together meant everything. I've never felt more drawn to a man in my life.

"Get up, Dylan," I say as I begin another pep talk to myself. "You have years of accumulated stuff to clean out." I groan at the realization that when I'm done with my office, I still have to clean out my mother's office. Dad and I couldn't stand the thought of her office being touched after she passed away. We just closed the door and have only entered it when there was a file we thought might be in there.

It's four in the afternoon. My coat is on, my purse is over my shoulder, and I'm about to walk out when Dad comes into my office.

"Wow, you've really cleaned out."

"Yeah, I'm just ready to get it over with," I say while

pulling out my car keys. When I pick up the box of pictures, Dad takes it away from me and sets it back down.

"Is there something I should know? You didn't even look at the contract or wait for Mr. Brown's attorney to explain it." He gives me that look he always does when he already knows the answer.

"I might… have… had a thing with Mr. Brown, but it's over now. Nothing to worry about."

He raises his eyebrows. When his hands land on his hips, I'm expecting him to be upset—but it's the opposite. "That might make things complicated and uncomfortable, since you're now working together," he comments.

"What are you talking about?" I fold my arms across my chest and wait for him to answer. He doesn't reply, which makes me a little worried. "Dad, what are you saying? Working together like you and me, or who?" My heart starts pounding and I feel myself getting agitated.

He lets out a deep breath. "If you would have taken the time to read the new contract, it says we're in a partnership. He's not buying the company. He's buying *into* the company!" Dad says excitedly.

"I thought you were ready to let it go?"

He teeters his head from side to side. "For a while, I thought I would like to retire. But when Shane approached me with his new offer, I realized that staying is exactly what I want. I love coming to work every day. What I didn't love was the worry about how we'd continue. Now we'll be able to save everyone's jobs and not feel the impact of our family business being torn to shreds." He looks at me thoughtfully. "I have a feeling you had something to do with his revised offer."

"Dad, I need to go." I kiss his cheek before I turn and almost run out the door.

CHAPTER TEN

Shane

THE METALLIC CLANG OF THE BARBELL BEING racked into the J-hooks is satisfying. After my meeting with Richard Daniel, I went back to the office for a few hours, but my focus was shit. So I called Jackson and begged him to meet me at the gym. Since he'd made the same request of me while he and Candy were figuring things out, I thought it was only fair to turn it around. Because there's nothing that burns off anxious energy and frustration like benching a bar loaded with forty-fives. Running on the treadmill until sweat drips off of you onto the belt is a close second.

"That sucks ass," Jackson spits out as he begins unloading the bar while I set up the bench for incline presses.

"Yeah, she wasn't there for any of the contract review. Just came in toward the end of the meeting, signed the contract without even glancing at it, then ran out of the room." He gives me a low whistle of commiseration. "Fuck, Jackson. Is this how chicks feel when we don't call them the next day?"

Jackson chuckles, "It's the boomerang effect." I must look confused because he raises his eyebrows and explains, "You know? When they fuck you and then get dressed and leave you a few dollars by the bedside table."

I look at him horrified, "Has that shit ever happened to you?"

He shrugs a shoulder, "Just once. Except I'm a pretty good fuck so it was more than a hundred." His shit eating grin tells me it was really just a few dollars.

"I'm out of my element here. No woman has ever made me want to beg for forgiveness like Dylan does." We move to the treadmills to finish up our workout.

"Welcome to my world. Candy has me in knots. When I don't hear from her, I start checking my phone to see where she is. Worrying over someone all the time sucks, but being with Candy is also the greatest thing that has ever happened to me. I wouldn't have it any other way." His eyes seem to shine more brightly now that he's talking about Candy.

I increase the pace and incline on my treadmill, trying to wear myself out. I need to go home exhausted or else I'll just sit and keep thinking of questionable ways to get Dylan to talk to me. The best I've come up with so far is having her kidnapped and tied to a chair—while appealing in more ways than one, it probably would only make her angrier. And I wouldn't want to worry her father. I actually like Richard. I went back to the board room after my disastrous confrontation with Dylan in the hallway, and he and I spoke for some time. He wants Dylan to pursue her dreams as much as I do… I just need to find a way to let her know that. "Maybe I should just give her space for now."

"I wouldn't wait too long. Space can be a funny thing. It could give someone else the chance to move in," he says, a little breathless.

"Well…" I pause my thought to turn the speed down so I'll be able to finish without hyperventilating. "I'll knock someone the fuck out if they try to touch her."

We wrap up our workout and hit the showers. Once we are done, Jackson gets a call from Mitchell. He wants him to meet up at the club he owns.

"You going?" Jackson asks me.

"Sure." I shrug, because it beats going home. I'd given William the day off and driven myself to my meeting at Daniel Advertising, sure that once we'd signed the contract I'd be taking Dylan home with me for a celebratory fuck. So I had a car… just no Dylan. "I'll meet you there."

It takes about twenty minutes to get to the club. When we arrive, Mitchell is waiting for us in the usual booth, along with Harrison. Jackson slides onto the bench beside Mitchell; I join Harrison on the opposite bench.

"You guys look like shit," Mitchell greets us, leading with his usual bullshit.

Harrison sits back, scoping out a new girl Mitchell has hired.

"Don't even think about it," Mitchell warns him when Harrison licks his lips as he checks out her ass.

Harrison raises his eyebrows to Mitchell, "You calling dibs?"

Mitchell growls, "She's off limits."

"Sounds like you got a boner for her," Harrison teases. Mitchell clenches his fist, barely holding himself back from jumping over the table to throttle Harrison.

"What the hell, man!" Jackson holds Mitchell back.

"That's my baby sister," Mitchell grinds out between his teeth.

Harrison's eyes go wide as he looks from Mitchell to his sister. "Why in the hell would you allow her to work here?"

"She needed a job and I needed to make sure no asshole messed with her. I'm letting one of them know now." Mitchell pointed his index finger at Harrison. "Don't mess with her."

My neck hurts from watching the interaction between the two, so I throw down a hundred and call it an early night. When I get into my car, my first instinct is to head over to Dylan's, but I decide against it and head to my penthouse.

I park my car in my space in the garage, walk over to the elevator and punch in the code. When the doors open to my penthouse, my dick plumps up in my slacks at the sight of Dylan standing in my foyer. She's wearing the same red skirt and crop top she had on when she cooked dinner for me at her house. Except this time, she's holding a sprig of mistletoe at her waistline.

"Hi," she whispers as she bats her eyes at me.

"Hey," I whisper back, my heart racing at the sight of her. My feet fly to where she's standing and then I'm looking down at the beautiful creature in front of me. "Have you been waiting long?" I don't care that she's, once again, somehow gotten past security since she's exactly where she needs to be.

"Just a little bit," she breaths.

We stand there breathing each other in. Being this close to her is where I always want to be. "Did your dad tell you about the contract?"

"Yes," her chest heaves. It appears that being close to me is having the same effect on her as it is on me. "Thank you."

"I would do anything for you, Dylan. Anything."

She rises on her tiptoes to whisper, "Then kiss me under the mistletoe."

I glance down to see that she's still holding the sprig of greenery. I drop to my knees and waste no time before diving in to consume every inch of her that's under the mistletoe.

Shane

EPILOGUE

Three Years Later

"Damn it!" I shout. "This shit has to stop."

I hear Dylan say, "What did you do?" Her voice came from the kitchen, so I stomp in that direction. Dylan is standing by the counter, chopping vegetables for our dinner, while Skyler and Mittens lay at her feet. Mittens lifts his head to growl at me, but Skyler just lays there, dozing, not a fucking care in the world.

"You!" I point at Skyler, who opens one eye to look at me. "You took a shit in my new Berluti shoes!"

"I'm sure he didn't mean to… you know he has bowel issues." Dylan defends the dog from hell, but her giggle and Mitten's bark from his new position at my feet let me know they're all against me having nice shoes.

I weave my way around the dogs until I'm behind her, then wrap my arms around her and rest them on her swollen belly. She's just started her final year of vet school and now we're expecting our first baby.

"How's our boy doing?"

"He's been kicking so hard today that I think we may have a professional soccer player in the making."

"That's my son," I chuckle as I rub her stomach. "I also think you owe me something for letting your dog take a shit in my shoe."

"Oh really." I can feel her smiling.

"Umm hmm."

She sets her knife on the counter and turns around in my arms, "I think I may need more details on what you are expecting, Mr. Brown."

"Well, Mrs. Brown, I think I should show you, and it'd be better in the bedroom with you on your knees."

"What if I can't *get* on my knees right now? What would you have me do?"

"I'll let you sit on the edge of the bed while I punish that mouth of yours with my cock. Would that work?" She teeters her head from side to side, as if contemplating my proposal. So I sweeten the deal. "Then I'll lay you back and lick that swollen clit of yours until you come in my mouth." As I talk, I start pulling her to the bedroom where I plan to make good on my promises.

Skyler gets his big body up and follows behind her. He's become overly protective of Dylan since she became pregnant, which I'm grateful for—but not when I plan on making her scream from pleasure.

"No, Skyler, no. Stay." The dog doesn't listen. He keeps following behind Dylan. "Dylan, tell him to stay."

She laughs. I mumble, "We really need boundaries in this house."

"Stay, Skyler," Dylan gently commands.

"Come here, woman," I growl as I pull her to me while using my foot to slam the door in Skyler's face. "I love you," I whisper against her lips before I take them with mine.

Also by Aurelia Yates

Dark Romance

Emerald Eyes
Sapphire Eyes
Amber Eyes

Contemporary Romance

Sparks Fly
Sparks Ignite
What Should Have Been
Professor Cane

About the Author

Aurelia writes dark and contemporary romance and enjoys reading it just as much! She lives in Alabama with her husband, daughter, and fur babies. She spends most of her time caring for her loved ones and plotting stories. She's excited to share her stories and to grow as an author. Look for more outstanding stories from Aurelia by following her on social media.

Follow Aurelia

https://www.goodreads.com/author/show/22689072.
Aurelia_Yates

https://www.bookbub.com/profile/aurelia-yates

https://www.facebook.com/aureliayatesauthor

https://www.instagram.com/aureliayatesauthor/

https://www.tiktok.com/@aureliayatesauthor